Keep Positive Thoughts!
Nikiyah Crosdale

Dedicated to my mother, father, and children all across the world.

Printed in the United States of America

First Printing, 2021

ISBN 978-1-7364417-0-1

Born You Publishing
P.O Box 16141
Kansas City, MO 64112S
www.BornYou.com

THE THOUGHT JAR

WRITTEN BY: NIKIYAH CROSDALE
ILLUSTRATED BY: DECARSO CARROLL

Hey Guys! My name is Ebea and today's the big day!

I have a spelling bee that I have been preparing for, for three whole weeks. I was excited up until last night.

I was up all night tossing and turning, thinking about all the bad things that could go wrong.

Like, what if it rains on my walk to school and I get soaked? or what if I eat something bad at lunch and puke all over the stage during the spelling bee?

I just knew today was going to be a bad day.

As I walked outside, I blew a sigh of relief. Even though it had stormed really bad last night, the sun was shining, and the sky was blue.

As I stood at the bus stop waiting for my bus to arrive, I thought, *this isn't so bad,* when all of a sudden, a car came zooming by, and splash!

The water from a huge pothole in the street soaked me from head to toe.

I just knew today would be a bad day, I thought as my bus pulled up.

The day was going fast and my nerves about the spelling bee kept getting worse and worse.

As I was walking to get my lunch in my damp clothes from the splash earlier, all I could think about was the spelling bee turning into a disaster.

After all, I did think about getting soaked before school and that came true.

What if I eat something that upsets my stomach and during the spelling bee, I puke all on the stage just like I imagined last night? How embarrassing will that be? I thought.

I reached to grab the lunch tray, but thought, I'm not going to take the risk; I'll just wait until after the spelling bee to eat.

As I sat at my table watching all my friends eat, my stomach started to rumble of hunger. This was turning out to be an awfully bad day, just as I had thought it would.

A few hours had passed, and it was finally time for the big spelling bee I had spent the last few weeks practicing for.

What if something goes wrong?
What if I forget all the words I practiced?
What if I trip and fall off the stage?
What if? What if? What if?

All of a sudden, every bad thought I could think of came rushing in. I wanted to crawl under a rock and never come out until all of this was over.

This was it!

"Spell 'achieve,'" said Mrs. Carey.

By this time, we were down to the final three contestants and so far I was doing great!

As I started to walk to the mic my hunger pains came rushing back.

"Achieve," I repeated as my stomach started to growl uncontrollably.

"A-C—" (roar)

I put my hand on my stomach hoping it would ease the pain, but that didn't work.

"H-E," I said as my voice started to shake, "I-V-E. Achieve," I said quickly, hoping to hurry this painful and embarrassing process up.

That is incorrect," said Mrs. Carey.

"The correct spelling is a-c-h-i-e-v-e."

I knew it!

That was one of the words I spent the longest time practicing. If I would have taken my time, I would have been able to move on to the final round. I put my head down, holding back my tears, and walked slowly off the stage.

Today was the worst day ever, just like I thought it would be.

It was the end of the day, and I was still saddened at the fact I didn't win the spelling bee.

Mrs. Carey called me over to her desk as I was walking to get my backpack.

"I've noticed you've been sad all day. Is everything ok?" she asked.

"No!" I replied.

"I just knew today would turn out to be a bad day. I was up all night tossing and turning thinking about all the things that could go wrong today. Not only did things go wrong, they were 10 times worse," I said.

"Interesting," replied Mrs. Carey, as if she already knew the solution to my problem.

"Ebea, do you know that you have the power to control whether you have a good day or a bad day?" she asked.

"No!" I replied as I wiped away my tears.

"So are you saying I am the reason I had a bad day?" I asked.

"Yes," Mrs. Carey replied...

"You have the power to think good or bad thoughts. Your thoughts and your feelings about something can control whether you have a good day or a bad day...

"Your thoughts can control how you feel. Your feelings are like magnets that will pull events in your life that matches the way you feel. So, you see Ebea," she said,

"you thought today would be a bad day, which led you to feel bad, so things went wrong to match your bad feelings."

It all started to click!

What Mrs. Carey was saying was right.

I stayed up all night thinking about all the bad things that could go wrong, and even though they didn't happen exactly the way I thought they would, things did go horribly wrong.

Mrs. Carey was right, everything that happened to me began with how I was thinking.

Mrs. Carey then reached over to a cool jar on her desk. It was covered in green, yellow, and blue glitter and on top of the glitter were stickers.

"You see, Ebea," said Mrs. Carey,

"I was just like you when I was about your age. I would have bad days and come home crying almost every day after school, until one day my mom and I decorated this jar. We called it The Thought Jar. Every night before bed I would think about something good that I wanted to happen, write it down, and put it in the jar. It was almost like magic. I was putting out good thoughts so good things started happening, and my days got better and better. I kept this jar this whole time because it works, and if it works for me it will work for you."

I smiled and thanked Mrs.Carey for her great advice.

Later that night, I asked my mom if I could use one of her old, recycled mason jars. I took out my art supplies and wrote on a piece of paper 'My Thought Jar' and glued it to the jar. I decorated the jar with shiny glitter of my favorite colors and stickers, just like Mrs.Carey's jar.

My thought jar was going to be amazing and all I needed was paper, a pencil, and some good thoughts.

Tomorrow will be a great day! I wrote down on a piece of paper, folded it up and placed it in my thought jar.

I immediately started feeling really good about tomorrow.

I started to think about all the good things that could happen.

Like...what if they serve my favorite meal, pizza, for lunch? Or what if Mrs. Carey decides to give us extra free time during recess?

"Tomorrow is going to be a great day!" I said to myself as I slowly closed my eyes and went to sleep.

The next morning, I woke up excited and ready to get my day started. I just knew today was going to be a great day.

Even though it was raining out, I didn't let that get me down; my umbrella kept me dry.

I was smiling from ear to ear all the way to my bus stop.

I thought back to what Mrs. Carey said, *I had the power to control whether I have a good day or a bad day by the way I thought.*

I was so excited to get to class to tell Mrs. Carey all about my thought jar.

As soon as I entered, I saw the class
          decorated with cool colors and balloons.

"Today we're having a surprise pizza party for
all the hard work and studying you all did for
the spelling bee,"said Mrs. Carey.

I instantly thought, *Wow! My thought jar actually worked.*

The entire day was full of laughter, fun, games, and my favorite food, pizza!

It was everything I could have imagined and more.

"Today is turning out to be a great day, just like I thought it would," I said to myself as I slid down the slide on the playground.

Each night I wrote a positive thought down and put it in my thought jar right before bed.

From that day forward, my days got better and better.

CREATE YOUR OWN THOUGHT JAR

Step 1: With adult supervision in clean jar pour 1/4 cup of polycrylic.
Step 2: Add lid. Shake in circular motion until entire inside of jar is covered in polycrylic.
Step 3: Remove lid. Pour remaining polycrylic back into can.
Step 4: Turn jar upside down on newspaper or towel for 3 mintutes to drain remaining polycrylic.
Step 5: Turn jar right side up, add glitter of your choice and design.
Step 6: Remove remaining glitter on newspaper or towel if necessary.
Step 7: Add stickers.
Step 8: Allow glitter to dry for 2 hours with no lid.
Step 9: You're all done! Grab paper, a pencil, and some good thoughts!

Materials Needed:

clean empty clear jar
newspaper or old towel
glitter
water based clear polycrylic
stickers

Parental/adult supervision required

The Thought Jar Exercise

1. Why did Ebea start off having a bad day?
    A. She didn't want to go to school
    B. She was up all-night thinking about all the things that could go wrong
    C. She had a bad headahe

2. Why did Ebea skip lunch?
    A. She didn't like what they were serving
    B. She thought she would get sick and puke during the spelling bee
    C. She wasn't hungry

3. What did Mrs. Carey do when she was a child to turn her bad days into good days?
    A. She started being nice to everyone
    B. She created a thought jar, wrote out a good thought and put it in the jar every night
    C. She cried everyday until her bad days turned into good days

4. Mrs. Carey said Ebea's___were like magnets that would pull events in her life that matched the way she felt.
    A. Outfits
    B. Feelings
    C. Shoes

5. What changed that made Ebea have a great day?
    A. She changed the way she thought about things
    B. She changed her bus stop
    C. She changed her outfit

6. Ebea instantly felt good when she thought about getting extra time to play during recess and eating her favorite food, pizza. What are some thoughts that you've had that made you feel good when thinking about them?

Made in the USA
Middletown, DE
08 August 2022

70658005R00033